BROWNIE & PEARL Take a Dip

by CYNTHIA RYLANT ❋ pictures by BRIAN BIGGS

Beach Lane Books

New York London Toronto Sydney

It is a hot day.
Brownie and Pearl
are going to take a dip.

Brownie finds her swimsuit.
Pearl finds her beach ball.

Don't forget sunglasses!

The pool is outside.
It is a small blue pool.

It is just the right size.

Brownie sticks a toe in.
Pearl does too.
Ooh, feels **nice**.

Brownie steps in.
Pearl does too.
Ooh, feels **very nice.**

Uh-oh!

Pearl takes a little swim.

Pearl is very, very, very **wet**.
She's ready to get out now.

She looks a little silly.
Brownie giggles.

Brownie giggles and giggles.

Pearl dries off in the sun.

Brownie stops giggling.
She gets out and dries off
in the sun too.

Ooh, that was a **nice** dip.

For Tarzan—B. B.

BEACH LANE BOOKS
An imprint of Simon & Schuster Children's Publishing Division
1230 Avenue of the Americas, New York, New York 10020
Text copyright © 2011 by Cynthia Rylant
Illustrations copyright © 2011 by Brian Biggs
BEACH LANE BOOKS is a trademark of Simon & Schuster, Inc.
For information about special discounts for bulk purchases, please contact Simon & Schuster Special Sales
at 1-866-506-1949 or business@simonandschuster.com.
The Simon & Schuster Speakers Bureau can bring authors to your live event. For more information or to book an event,
contact the Simon & Schuster Speakers Bureau at 1-866-248-3049 or visit our website at www.simonspeakers.com.
Book design by Sonia Chaghatzbanian
The text for this book is set in Berliner Grotesk.
The illustrations for this book are rendered digitally.
Manufactured in China
0111 SCP
First Edition
2 4 6 8 10 9 7 5 3 1
Library of Congress Cataloging-in-Publication Data
Rylant, Cynthia.
Brownie & Pearl take a dip / by Cynthia Rylant ; illustrated by Brian Biggs.—1st ed.
p. cm.
Summary: One hot day, a little girl and her cat enjoy a backyard pool.
ISBN 978-1-4169-8638-6 (hardcover)
[1. Swimming pools—Fiction. 2. Cats—Fiction.] I. Biggs, Brian, ill. II. Title. III. Title: Brownie and Pearl take a dip.
PZ7.R982Btm 2011
[E]—dc22
2009032468